A Note to Parents and Caregivers:

Read-it! Readers are for children who are just starting on the amazing road to reading. These beautiful books support both the acquisition of reading skills and the love of books.

 The PURPLE LEVEL presents basic topics and objects using high frequency words and simple language patterns.

 The RED LEVEL presents familiar topics using common words and repeating sentence patterns.

 The BLUE LEVEL presents new ideas using a larger vocabulary and varied sentence structure.

 The YELLOW LEVEL presents more challenging ideas, a broad vocabulary, and wide variety in sentence structure.

 The GREEN LEVEL presents more complex ideas, an extended vocabulary range, and expanded language structures.

 The ORANGE LEVEL presents a wide range of ideas and concepts using challenging vocabulary and complex language structures.

When sharing a book with your child, read in short stretches, pausing often to talk about the pictures. Have your child turn the pages and point to the pictures and familiar words. And be sure to reread favorite stories or parts of stories.

There is no right or wrong way to share books with children. Find time to read with your child, and pass on the legacy of literacy.

Adria F. Klein, Ph.D.
Professor Emeritus
California State University
San Bernardino, California

Editor: Christianne Jones
Designer: Amy Muehlenhardt
Page Production: Michelle Biedscheid
Art Director: Nathan Gassman
The illustrations in this book were created in watercolor and pencil.

Picture Window Books
5115 Excelsior Boulevard
Suite 232
Minneapolis, MN 55416
877-845-8392
www.picturewindowbooks.com

Printed in the United States of America in Stevens Point, Wisconsin.
072009
005594R

All books published by Picture Window Books
are manufactured with paper containing at least
10 percent post-consumer waste.

Library of Congress Cataloging-in-Publication Data
Klein, Adria F. (Adria Fay), 1947-
Max goes to the doctor / by Adria F. Klein ; illustrated by Mernie Gallagher-Cole.
p. cm. — (Read-it! readers. The life of Max)
Summary: When it is time for his yearly checkup, Max goes to the doctor and gets
very good news.
ISBN-13: 978-1-4048-3680-8 (library binding)
ISBN-10: 1-4048-3680-2 (library binding)
ISBN-13: 978-1-4048-3686-0 (paperback)
ISBN-10: 1-4048-3686-1 (paperback)
[1. Physicians—Fiction. 2. Medical care—Fiction.] I. Gallagher-Cole, Mernie, ill.
II. Title.
PZ7.K678324Maq 2007
[E]—dc22   2007004051

Max
Goes to the
Doctor

by Adria F. Klein
illustrated by Mernie Gallagher-Cole

Special thanks to our advisers for their expertise:

Adria F. Klein, Ph.D.
Professor Emeritus, California State University
San Bernardino, California

Susan Kesselring, M.A., Literacy Educator
Rosemount–Apple Valley–Eagan (Minnesota) School District

PICTURE WINDOW BOOKS
Minneapolis, Minnesota

Max is going to the doctor. It is time for his yearly checkup.

He wants to stay healthy.

The doctor checks how tall Max is.

Max has grown two inches. This is good.

The doctor checks how much Max weighs.

Max has gained five pounds. This is good.

The doctor checks Max's blood pressure.

The doctor says it's like giving Max's arm a hug.

The doctor listens to Max's heart. It has a strong beat.

It beats eighty times in one minute.
This is good.

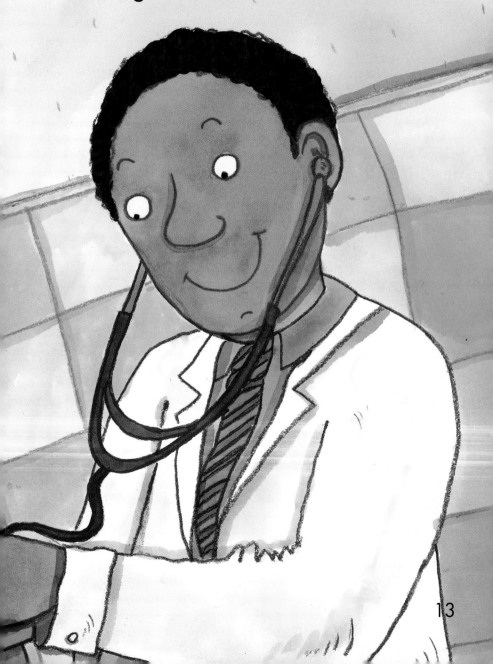

The doctor looks in Max's ears and eyes.

They both look healthy. This is good.

The doctor takes Max's temperature.

It is 98.6 degrees Fahrenheit. This is good.

The doctor gives Max two shots. The
shots will help him stay healthy.

Max holds his mom's hand. He does not cry.

The doctor gives Max a sticker for being brave.

Max had a great checkup. He is
very healthy.

More *Read-it!* Readers

Bright pictures and fun stories help you practice your reading skills. Look for more books at your level.

Max Goes on the Bus
Max Goes Shopping
Max Goes to School
Max Goes to the Barber
Max Goes to the Dentist
Max Goes to the Library
Max Goes to the Playground
Max Goes to the Zoo

Max and Buddy Go to the Vet
Max and the Adoption Day Party
Max Celebrates Chinese New Year
Max Goes to a Cookout
Max Goes to the Farm
Max Goes to the Grocery Store
Max Learns Sign Language
Max Stays Overnight
Max's Fun Day

On the Web

FactHound offers a safe, fun way to find Web sites related to this book. All of the sites on FactHound have been researched by our staff.

1. Visit www.facthound.com
2. Type in this special code: 1404836802
3. Click on the FETCH IT button.

Your trusty FactHound will fetch the best sites for you!
A complete list of *Read-it!* Readers is available on our Web site:
www.picturewindowbooks.com